THE SILVER SIX

BY AJ LIEBERMAN & DARREN RAWLINGS

graphix

An Imprint of

SCHOLASTIC

For Hannah & Rebecca:
my Silver Two!
AJL

Dedicated to my wife and children,
for their unrelenting patience in having their
husband and father constantly cooped up in his office,
seemingly working hard at drawing cartoons
and comics all day long.
Rawls

Text copyright © 2013 by AJ Lieberman
Illustrations copyright © 2013 by Darren Rawlings

All rights reserved. Published by Graphix, a division of Scholastic Inc., *Publishers since 1920.* SCHOLASTIC, GRAPHIX, and associated logos are trademarks and/or registered trademarks of Scholastic Inc.

Library of Congress Control Number: 2012945144

ISBN 978-0-545-37097-4
ISBN 978-0-545-37098-1 (paperback)

10 9 8 7 6 5 4 3 2 1   13 14 15 16 17
Printed in China   38

First edition, July 2013
Edited by Adam Rau
Book design by Phil Falco
Creative Director: David Saylor

THIS BETTER BE VERY, *VERY* GOOD.

MR. CRAVEN, SOMEONE ON THAT SHUTTLE SENT A FILE RIGHT BEFORE IT EXPLODED.

LET ME HAVE IT.

OKAY, WELL, HERE'S THE THING...

BEFORE I COULD DOWNLOAD IT, THE CONNECTION WAS LOST DUE TO THE EXPLOSION.

WHAT?!

WHAT'S YOUR NAME?

D-DAVE.

LISTEN TO ME VERY CAREFULLY, DAVE.

I WANT YOU TO DROP EVERYTHING AND FIND OUT WHERE THAT FILE WAS SENT.

BECAUSE YOU'RE NOT LEAVING UNTIL YOU DO.

B-BUT I DON'T KNOW IF IT'S EVEN POSSIBLE TO--

WAIT... WHEN YOU SAY I'M NOT LEAVING YOU DON'T LITERALLY MEAN I'M NOT--

'CAUSE I'M 85% SURE I FORGOT TO FEED MY FISH THIS MORNING AND--

BY THE END OF THE DAY!

ONE YEAR LATER

I LIVE SOMEWHERE DOWN THERE, IN AN AREA CALLED "THE BUBBLES."

A LONG, LONG TIME AGO, MAYBE EVEN LONGER THAN THAT, PEOPLE CALLED IT BOSTON.

BUT NOW EVERYONE I KNOW CALLS IT THE BUBBLES.

WHICH SOUNDS KINDA CUTE AND CHARMING, BUT IT'S NOT CUTE AND NOT AT ALL CHARMING.

IT'S WHAT MY DAD WOULD HAVE CALLED IRONIC.

MY MOM JUST CALLED IT DEPRESSING.

AND ME? I CALL IT HOME.

FOR NOW.

5

I'M MAD AT YOU.

GO AWAY, MAX.

I'M SERIOUS. I'M MAD AT YOU.

I'M SERIOUS, TOO. GO AWAY.

I WANT TO SLEEP.

YOU WANT MS. DEROSA TO YELL AT YOU?

ABOUT WHAT?

BEING LATE. IT'S ALMOST EIGHT O'CLOCK.

WHAT?!

ALARM SYSTEMS MUST'VE GONE OFF LINE.

MAX...

...YOU'RE MY ALARM SYSTEM!

YOUR HARD DRIVE MUST BE SLIPPING AGAIN.

OKAY, I HAVE *NO* IDEA WHAT YOU'RE TALKING ABOUT.

MAX...

YOU'RE SUPPOSED TO MAKE MY LIFE EASIER, NOT HARDER.

WHY IS IT MY JOB?

BECAUSE YOU'RE MY ROBOT!

I'LL HAVE YOU KNOW THAT THOSE WORDS ARE BOTH CRUEL AND INSENSITIVE.

YOU'RE CRAZY.

KNOCK KNOCK KNOCK

MR. HEMINGWAY. IT'S THE LANDLORD! OPEN UP! WE NEED TO TALK!

MAX, WHEN I TOLD YOU TO TAKE THE RENT DOWN, DID YOU TAKE THE RENT DOWN?

YES.

THEN *WHY* IS THE LANDLORD BANGING ON OUR DOOR?!

...

OKAY, MAYBE I DIDN'T.

MAX!!

unch time

DINNER time - #

time For Bed - #

huRRy UP, LeTs Go

Mom angry @

homework done

Goodnight - #

Good morning

wake UP - #01

wake UP - #0

WHAT?! YOU KNOW I DON'T DO WELL UNDER PRESSURE.

APPARENTLY YOU DON'T DO WELL WITH *DIRECTIONS*, EITHER.

HERE, USE THESE.

Mom in Shower

rent - #04

NG okay?

READY?

GO.

HEY, KID. I NEED TO SPEAK TO YOUR DAD. HE IN?

PHOEBE, HAVE YOU SEEN MY SOCKS?

YEAH, NO. BIG MEETING.

CONFERENCE ROOM. HOLOGRAPHS. THERMAL CHARTS.

HE LEFT EARLY.

OOPS!

WHAT WAS-- WAS *THAT* YOUR FATHER?

MR. PETERSON.

WHAT?

MR. PETERSON IN 80-J. THIN WALLS. HAS A THING FOR SOCKS.

LOOK, KID, WE DO THIS DANCE EVERY TIME YOU'RE LATE WITH THE MONEY.

LAST TIME THEY WERE STUCK IN AN ELEVATOR, BEFORE THAT IT WAS TRAFFIC.

YOUR FOLKS AIN'T NEVER HOME, AND I'M NOT LEAVIN' TILL I SPEAK--

PHOEBE, IS THAT THE LANDLORD?

YEAH.

TELL HIM I'M IN THE SHOWER AND GIVE HIM THE RENT, OKAY?

MY MOM SAID SHE'S IN THE--

YEAH, I HEARD.

PHOEBE, EVERYTHING OKAY?

WELL, IS IT?

...FOR NOW.

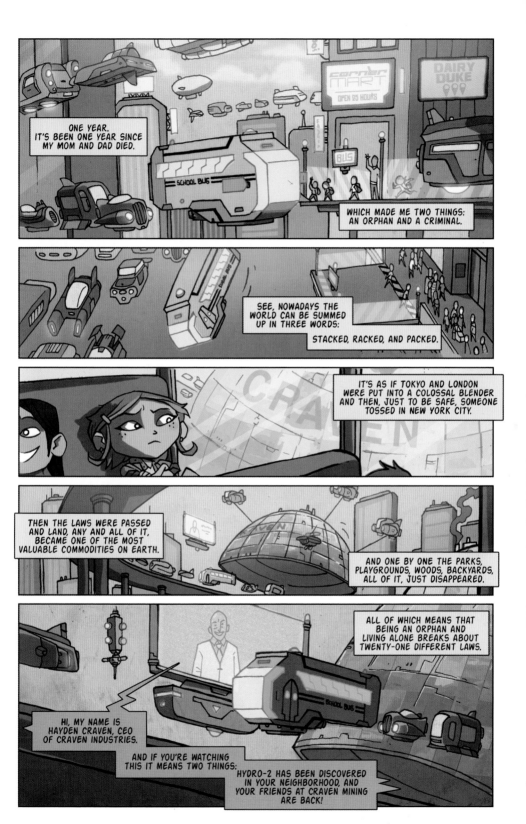

ONE YEAR. IT'S BEEN ONE YEAR SINCE MY MOM AND DAD DIED.

WHICH MADE ME TWO THINGS: AN ORPHAN AND A CRIMINAL.

SEE, NOWADAYS THE WORLD CAN BE SUMMED UP IN THREE WORDS:

STACKED, RACKED, AND PACKED.

IT'S AS IF TOKYO AND LONDON WERE PUT INTO A COLOSSAL BLENDER AND THEN, JUST TO BE SAFE, SOMEONE TOSSED IN NEW YORK CITY.

THEN THE LAWS WERE PASSED AND LAND, ANY AND ALL OF IT, BECAME ONE OF THE MOST VALUABLE COMMODITIES ON EARTH.

AND ONE BY ONE THE PARKS, PLAYGROUNDS, WOODS, BACKYARDS, ALL OF IT, JUST DISAPPEARED.

ALL OF WHICH MEANS THAT BEING AN ORPHAN AND LIVING ALONE BREAKS ABOUT TWENTY-ONE DIFFERENT LAWS.

HI, MY NAME IS HAYDEN CRAVEN, CEO OF CRAVEN INDUSTRIES.

AND IF YOU'RE WATCHING THIS IT MEANS TWO THINGS:

HYDRO-2 HAS BEEN DISCOVERED IN YOUR NEIGHBORHOOD, AND YOUR FRIENDS AT CRAVEN MINING ARE BACK!

WHICH MEANS LIFE IS ABOUT TO GET A WHOLE LOT BETTER...

...RIGHT AFTER IT GETS A LITTLE BIT WORSE.

WHAT...?

YOU'RE RIGHT. IT *IS* EXCITING NEWS!

CRAVEN MINING IS UNIQUELY QUALIFIED TO DRILL FOR HYDRO-2 BECAUSE WE PIONEERED THE LATEST IN EXCAVATION TECHNIQUES, LIKE...

DEEP-SOIL DRILLING.

SUB-SUBTERRANEAN DEMOLITION.

EXCAVATION TECHNIQUES

APPROVED

6 out of 5 SCIENTISTS APPROVE!

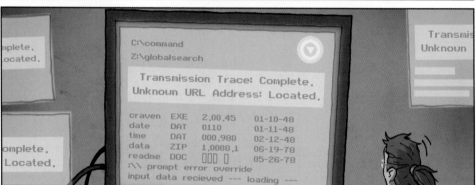

AGENT STUBBIN, YOU DO **NOT** HAVE THE RIGHT TO DISRUPT MY--

PRINCIPAL BRIGUGLIO, THIS BADGE GIVES ME THE RIGHT **AND** THE AUTHORITY.

I DON'T LIKE YOUR TONE, AGENT STUB--

I'D WORRY **LESS** ABOUT MY TONE AND **MORE** ABOUT WHAT'S GOING TO HAPPEN--

--WHEN MY BOSS ASKS YOUR BOSS ONE SIMPLE QUESTION:

HOW DID THE PRINCIPAL NOT KNOW SHE HAD AN ILLEGAL ORPHAN ATTENDING HER SCHOOL?

ARE YOU THREATENING ME?

ABSOLUTELY.

HOW LONG WAS THE ORPHAN ATTENDING SCHOOL?

WHAT ABOUT REPORT CARDS?

WAIT--

DIDN'T THE SCHOOL REQUIRE PARENT SIGNATURES?

AND PARENT/TEACHER CONFERENCES?

TWICE A YEAR, RIGHT?

WHAT ABOUT SICK NOTES?

SEE A PATTERN HERE?

THAT'S BLACKMAIL!

I KNOW.

OKAY! FINE!

SHE'S IN CLASS 34. I'LL SHOW YOU.

YOU THINKING WHAT I'M THINKING?

ARE YOU THINKING ABOUT PIZZA?

YES.

MAX!

WHAT? WHY?

WE GOTTA GET BACK IN THERE.

THAT MOON REGISTRY WAS THE LAST GIFT MOM AND DAD GAVE ME.

PHOEBS, I DON'T KNOW HOW THEY FOUND US, BUT THEY DID.

THEY HAVE TO BE WATCHING.

OR... THEY THINK WE'RE A THOUSAND MILES AWAY BY NOW.

OKAY, BUT I RAN THE NUMBERS.

WE HAVE A 98.8529% CHANCE OF GETTING CAUGHT.

WELL, THAT STILL GIVES US A CHANCE.

EITHER WAY, I'M NOT LEAVING WITHOUT THAT REGISTRY, MAX.

NOT FOR ANYTHING.

NOT EVEN IF IT MEANS I GET CAUGHT.

WHAT'S TAKING SO LONG?

HOLD ON. I'VE ALMOST GOT IT.

YOU GOTTA GET OUT OF THERE!

I KNOW! I JUST...

I WANNA LOOK AROUND. JUST ONE MORE TIME.

BYE...

PHOEBE HEMINGWAY.

YOU'RE IN A LOT OF TROUBLE.

Y-YEAH...?

CLICK

THEN I SHOULD PROBABLY RUN.

WAIT!

STOP!

ARE YOU TRYING TO *KILL* ME?!

TRUST ME, IF I WANTED YOU DEAD, I WOULDN'T HAVE MISSED.

29

RED 45-8965, PLEASE TAKE A SEAT.

M-MY NAME IS KEVIN.

NOT ANYMORE IT ISN'T.

WELCOME TO THE CHILD WELFARE SERVICES DORMITORY COMPOUND C, NORTH-EAST DIVISION.

WHILE A GUEST HERE YOU'LL BE EXPECTED TO DO FOUR THINGS AND FOUR THINGS ONLY.

EAT. SLEEP. STUDY. WORK.

IF YOU DO NOT STUDY OR WORK YOU WILL NOT EAT OR SLEEP.

IN THIS WAY YOU WILL HELP DEFRAY THE CONSIDERABLE COST TO THE STATE TO KEEP YOU HOUSED IN THIS FACILITY.

ANY QUESTIONS?

I DIDN'T THINK SO.

SILVER 67-987.

HEY, KID!

THIS IS YOU.

AND HERE'S YOUR BUNK ASSIGNMENT.

WHAT IS THIS?

ROOKIE?

YEAH.

SUPPOSED TO KEEP US CALM.

DOES IT WORK?

YOU'LL FIND OUT.

LOST?

I HOPE SO.

WHERE DO YA WANNA BE?

QUAD 6, LEVEL 3...?

MY NAME'S HANNAH YOSHIYAMA.

PHOEBE.

OKAY, IT'S A GOOD NEWS/BAD NEWS THING.

WHAT DO YOU WANT FIRST?

I COULD USE SOME GOOD NEWS.

YOU'RE THE THIRD POD. THE THREES HAVE THE BEST MATTRESSES.

THAT'S THE GOOD NEWS?

WHAT'S THE BAD NEWS?

YOU'RE HERE.

THIS IS YOU.

FOR WHAT IT'S WORTH, THE FIRST NIGHT IS THE HARDEST.

THE LONGER YOU STAY, THE EASIER IT GETS.

THEN I HOPE IT NEVER GETS EASIER.

CLICK

...

I MISS YOU BOTH *SO* MUCH...

WHERE WE AT, PATEL?

FIVE...

FOUR...

THREE...

TWO...

ONE...

AAAND...

WRA WRA WRA WRA WRA

ZZZZ

WAM!

NEVER GETS OLD.

Ha Ha Ha

HE HE

HAW

THEY LOVE TO SEE THE NEW KIDS DO THAT. SORRY.

THIS IS REBECCA. BECCA, MEET PHOEBE.

IT'S OKAY. HI.

YOU HUNGRY?

STARVING.

THAT'S TOO BAD.

WHAT IS **THIS?**

THAT'S YOUR BREAKFAST.

NO, NO. I ORDERED OATMEAL WITH STRAWBERRIES AND A MUFFIN.

KISS TH CHE

YEAH, THAT'S WHAT YOU HAVE.

THOSE ARE THE STRAWBERRIES.

THE SOONER YOU ACCEPT THAT THIS IS YOUR LIFE,

THE EASIER IT GETS.

HELLO.

YOU'VE MET OLIVER AND PATEL. THIS IS IAN.

F.B.S., HUH?

BIG-TIME.

HOW YOU DOING?

W-WE'RE, LIKE, FORTY STORIES UP!!

ACTUALLY, FIFTY, BUT I SEE YOUR POINT.

FIFTY STORIES!?!

ARE YOU INSANE?!

ARE THEY INSANE?!

WHAT'S NEXT? SWIMMING THE SEWER SYSTEM?!

ACTUALLY, THE YELLOWS DO THE SEWERS.

CHILD WELFARE SERVICES

BESIDES, IT CAN GET A LOT WORSE.

OH. REALLY?! WHAT COULD BE WORSE?!

SCHOOL.

CAN ANYONE TELL US THE NAMES OF COLUMBUS'S SHIPS?

OKAY, SO LAST WEEK WE LEFT OFF AT CHRISTOPHER COLUMBUS.

ANYONE...? COLUMBUS'S THREE SHIPS?

PEOPLE, THIS WILL BE ON THE FINAL.

THE *MARY ANN*.

THE *INVINCIBLE*.

AND, OF COURSE, THE *MILLENNIUM FALCON*.

IS THIS A JOKE?

TELL ME HE'S JOKING.

TRUST ME, LET IT GO.

LET IT-- NO, THIS IS--

EXCUSE ME! HELLO?! THAT'S NOT RIGHT. THOSE AREN'T THE RIGHT NAMES.

REALLY?

YES, REALLY.

BECAUSE YOU KNOW WHAT I HAVE THAT YOU DO NOT?

THE ANSWER BOOK.

AND YOU KNOW WHY I HAVE THE ANSWER BOOK?

BECAUSE I'M THE *TEACHER!*

YOU'RE WRONG.

HE'S WRONG.

IT'S THE *NIÑA*, THE *PINTA*, AND THE *SANTA MARIA*.

RIIIGHT.

WHAT'S YOUR NUMBER, SILVER?

MY *NAME* IS PHOEBE HEMINGWAY.

SERIOUSLY, PHOEBE, IT'S NOT WORTH IT.

NEXT YOU'LL BE TELLING US THAT COLUMBUS WASN'T SEARCHING FOR NEW TRADE ROUTES TO CLEVELAND.

WHAT?! NO, *INDIA*. HE WAS LOOKING FOR *INDIA*.

REALLY?

BECAUSE THAT'S, LIKE, THE TOTAL OPPOSITE DIRECTION.

YOU THINK A GUY LIKE COLUMBUS WOULD MAKE THAT BIG OF A MISTAKE?

PSSST.

IS THIS GUY FOR REAL?

YOU THINK THEY GET THE BEST AND BRIGHTEST FOR CHILD WELFARE KIDS?

PSSSSSSST.

PSSST.

ZZZZ

MAX?!

WHAT ARE YOU DOING HERE?

WHO IS THIS?

HE'S MY HOUSE BOT!

HOW DID YOU GET IN HERE?

I GOT A JOB. I'M AN EDU-BOT FOR YOUR TEACHER.

I GRADE THE PAPERS AND TESTS AND STUFF.

MAX, YOU'RE NOT PROGRAMMED TO DO--

IS THAT WHY HE SAID CLEVELAND?!

HEY, WATCH YOUR TONE. I CAN FAIL YOU IF I WANT.

MAX!

I GOTTA GO. BUT I BROUGHT YOU THIS.

OPEN IT LATER.

OKAY, THIS IS KINDA WEIRD...

WAIT. THERE'S MORE.

C'MON, OLIVER, SHE SHOWED YOU HERS, NOW YOU SHOW HER YOURS.

HAPPY?

OKAY, NOW THIS IS WHATEVER COMES AFTER WEIRD.

SO WE ALL HAVE THE SAME THING. IT'S A GAG GIFT.

THEN HOW DO YOU EXPLAIN THAT?

HUH, THAT'S... NEW.

WHAT IS IT?

THERE MUST BE A MICROCHIP EMBEDDED IN THE PARCHMENT PAPER. PHOEBE'S REGISTRY MUST'VE COMPLETED THE CIRCUIT.

A MICROCHIP HOLDS INFORMATION. WE SHOULD FIND OUT WHAT'S ON THEM!

YOU GUYS ARE *CRAZY*. IT'S NOTHING. MAYBE THEY *CAME* LIKE THAT.

THEN WHY DIDN'T THEY GLOW BEFORE? WE SHOULD TRY AND OPEN THEM.

I DON'T THINK THAT'S A GOOD IDEA.

WHAT? WHY?

WHOEVER DID THIS WENT TO A LOT OF TROUBLE TO HIDE THEM, RIGHT?

THEY PROBABLY INCLUDED SOME KIND OF SECURITY DEFAULT.

WE DO IT WRONG, IT MIGHT ERASE THE MICROCHIPS.

YOU KNOW WHAT THIS MAKES US?

WHAT?

A TEAM!

WHAT ARE YOU TALKING ABOUT?

HOW DID IT GO?

GOT ALL MY VIDEOS.

THEY GOT MY GAME PLAYER.

HOW DID YOU GUYS MAKE OUT?

WE'VE GOT A PROBLEM.

THEY TOOK CAPTAIN VON DAZZLE.

WHO?

CAPTAIN VON-- MY UNICORN.

I HID MY REGISTRY INSIDE MY UNICORN, AND THE GUARDS TOOK HIM.

YET ANOTHER REASON TO HATE UNICORNS.

WHERE WOULD THEY HAVE TAKEN IT?

THE VAULT.

THAT AS SECURE AS IT SOUNDS?

ROTATING PASSWORD.

VIDEO SURVEILLANCE.

UNDERPAID ARMED GUARDS LOOKING FOR ANY EXCUSE TO FIRE THEIR WEAPONS.

IT'LL TAKE AT *LEAST* TWO WEEKS TO FIGURE A WAY IN.

WELL, THAT'S ONE THING WE HAVE:

TIME.

LATER

WE'RE OUTTA TIME.

WHAT ARE YOU TALKING ABOUT?

I WAS DOING SOME WORK ON THE ADMIN COMPUTER SYSTEM. SAW AN E-MAIL.

IT LOOKS LIKE THEY'RE GETTING READY FOR A DORM TRANSFER TO PHOENIX.

WHO?

SILVER AND RED. WE COULD BE SPLIT UP.

YOU KNOW WHAT THIS MEANS?

THE SILVER SIX ARE GOING INTO ACTION!

GIVE THE SILVER SIX THING A REST, OKAY?

EASE UP, OLIVER.

NO!

WE'RE NOT SOME BOGUS SUPERHERO TEAM, OKAY?

LOOK AROUND. THIS IS REAL.

WHICH IS **WHY** I'M NOT GOING TO SPEND THE NEXT FOUR YEARS,

FOUR MONTHS,

FOUR DAYS,

OR FOUR MINUTES IN HERE IF I CAN HELP IT!

OUT?!

AND GO **WHERE?**

WE **HAVE** NO PLACE TO GO!

ESPECIALLY IF THOSE MICROCHIPS MIGHT HELP US GET OUTTA HERE!

WE DO, TOO.

ARE YOU **SERIOUS?**

YEAH. WHY?

BECAUSE IT'S A JOKE!

IT'S A **GAG GIFT!**

SOMETHING YOUR PARENTS BUY WHEN THEY DON'T KNOW WHAT ELSE TO BUY YOU.

IT'S NOT.

IT'S MORE.

IS THAT CONCERN OR SELF-PRESERVATION I HEAR IN YOUR VOICE?

BOTH. NOW WHAT'S THE PLAN?

WE'VE ALREADY HACKED THE SECURITY SYSTEM AND ROUTED THEIR PHONE LINES.

ONCE WE TRIGGER THEIR ALARM THEY'LL CALL IT IN AND WE'LL SHOW UP.

ONCE INSIDE WE GRAB THE GIRL, BOLT, AND FLIP THE ALARM BACK ON.

TOP TO BOTTOM, MAYBE FOURTEEN MINUTES.

NO ONE IS GOING TO KNOW WE WERE EVEN THERE.

ARE YOU *KIDDING ME?*

WHAT IS IT WITH GIRLS AND UNICORNS?

THEY ARE A SYMBOL OF OUR CHILDHOOD. PLUS THEY'RE SUPERCUTE.

I GOT HIM. I'LL MEET YOU AT THE DOCKS.

MR. STRICK, LOOK! THERE SHE IS!

OOF!

HEY! WATCH IT!

THE
TRUCK!

THEY'RE ON
THAT TRUCK!

THIS IS TOTALLY FUN!

MAX!

WHAT NOW?

OVER HERE!

PATEL, LET'S GO!

OLIVER, LET'S GO!

WE'LL BE FINE.

REALLY...?

'CAUSE IF WE GET BUSTED, THE DORMS ARE GONNA FEEL LIKE AN AMUSEMENT PARK COMPARED TO WHERE THEY'RE GOING TO SEND US!

HE'S NOT GONNA GET US.

HOW DO YOU KNOW?!

BECAUSE I HAVE HIS SPARK PLUGS.

OKAY, SO WHERE TO?

OUR MOON! THE COORDINATES ARE ON THE REGISTRY.

WRRRR WRR...

LUCKY?!

THAT'S THE EXCUSE YOU'RE GOING WITH? LUCKY?!

THEY'RE KIDS!

CAN YOU HANDLE THIS?

YES.

THEN START ACTING LIKE IT!

THAT GIRL IS THE ONLY ONE WHO CAN CONNECT ME, YOU, AND THIS COMPANY TO THAT SHUTTLE EXPLOSION.

SHE CAN *DESTROY* THIS WHOLE COMPANY!

I'M *NOT* GOING TO LET THAT HAPPEN.

NOW HOW DO YOU PLAN ON FINDING HER?

THEY STOLE A CITY VEHICLE.

SO?

THAT'S MY BOY.

GO GET THEM.

ALL CITY VEHICLES ARE EQUIPPED WITH A TRACKING DEVICE.

AUTOPILOT DEACTIVATING. APPROACHING DESTINATION.

THAT'S IT?

UNLESS WE'RE TOTALLY LOST, THAT'S IT.

WOW... LOOK AT IT!

IT'S *MAGNIFICENT!*

WE'RE HOME.

I'M HUNGRY.

SO AM I.

ME TOO.

WE SHOULD PROBABLY ORGANIZE OUR SUPPLIES.

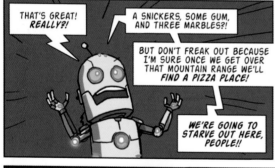

I HAVE A SNICKERS, TWO PIECES OF GUM, AND A SOCKET WRENCH.

A WHITE ERASER.

THREE MARBLES.

THAT'S GREAT! *REALLY?!*

A SNICKERS, SOME GUM, AND THREE MARBLES?!

BUT DON'T FREAK OUT BECAUSE I'M SURE ONCE WE GET OVER THAT MOUNTAIN RANGE WE'LL *FIND A PIZZA PLACE!*

WE'RE GOING TO STARVE OUT HERE, PEOPLE!!

ARE YOU DONE?

I BELIEVE I AM.

MAX IS RIGHT. WE SHOULD PROBABLY SEE HOW MUCH FOOD WE HAVE.

COULDN'T HURT TO LOOK AROUND.

AND WE SHOULD READ THE MICROCHIPS.

WHAT'S THE RUSH?

WE'RE GONNA BE HERE FOR A WHILE, RIGHT?

LET'S CHECK THIS PLACE OUT!

HOLD ON. AFTER ALL THIS TIME YOU GUYS AREN'T CURIOUS ABOUT THE MICROCHIPS?

HOW LONG WERE YOU LOCKED UP?

THREE WEEKS.

I WAS INSIDE FOR *ELEVEN* MONTHS!

HANNAH?

EIGHT.

IAN?

TEN.

PATEL?

NINE.

REBECCA?

TEN.

THREE WEEKS?

THIS IS THE FIRST TIME I'VE BEEN OUTSIDE WITHOUT A RENT-A-COP STANDING OVER ME IN ALMOST A YEAR!

THE CHIPS CAN WAIT.

WHAT DO YOU THINK WE SHOULD DO?

GET RID OF OLIVER.

WHAT?

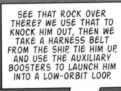

SEE THAT ROCK OVER THERE? WE USE THAT TO KNOCK HIM OUT, THEN WE TAKE A HARNESS BELT FROM THE SHIP, TIE HIM UP, AND USE THE AUXILIARY BOOSTERS TO LAUNCH HIM INTO A LOW-ORBIT LOOP.

WE'RE NOT DOING THAT.

WHATEVER.

THIS ISN'T HOW I THOUGHT IT'D BE.

HOW YOU THOUGHT WHAT WOULD BE?

EVERYTHING.

I WAS GLAD WHEN I FOUND THE OTHERS. EVEN WHILE I WAS LOCKED UP IN THE DORMS.

FOR THE FIRST TIME SINCE MOM AND DAD DIED I THOUGHT THINGS WERE GETTING BETTER.

BUT NOW IT'S JUST LIKE BEFORE. LIKE IT WAS BACK HOME.

ALONE.

...

YOU THINK HANNAH LIKES ME?

WHAT?!

WHEN WE WERE ON THE LOADING DOCKS, I FELT A CONNECTION. WILL YOU TALK TO HER FOR ME?

NO.

WHY?

BECAUSE YOU THINK I'M A ROBOT?

NO, BECAUSE I THINK YOU'RE CRAZY!

AT LEAST I'M NOT *CRYING* LIKE THE NERDY KID.

WHO?

THE GEEKY ONE WITH THE GLASSES.

IAN? HE'S NOT A GEEK--

WAIT... HE'S *CRYING?*

I AGREE.

REALLY?

YEAH.

YOU WANNA BRING YOUR SLEEPING BAG OVER TO MY AREA?

OF COURSE!

UHH...

CAN I JUST SAY IT'S, LIKE, *TOTALLY* DARK OUT THERE.

YOU GUYS CAN COME, TOO.

I MADE A FLAMELESS HEATER BASED ON AN EXOTHERMIC REACTION.

AND FOR THOSE OF US WHO ONLY SPEAK ENGLISH?

AN EXOTHERMIC REACTION IS A CHEMICAL REACTION THAT RELEASES ENERGY IN THE FORM OF HEAT.

AHH, WOULDN'T YOU NEED *CHEMICALS* TO HAVE A CHEMICAL REACTION?

CaO CALCIUM OXIDE

EXHIBIT A: CALCIUM OXIDE POWDER. THIS PLACE IS FULL OF IT.

EXHIBIT B: WATER. WHICH, WHEN ADDED TO THE POWDER, WILL CREATE A REACTION...

H_2O WATER

$H_2O + CaO$

$Ca(OH)_2$ CALCIUM HYDROXIDE & HEAT

...AND PRODUCE ENOUGH HEAT TO COOK ALMOST ANYTHING.

WHAT *I* WANT TO KNOW IS, WHO WAS THAT GUY AT THE DOCKS?

YEAH, THE GUY *SHOOTING* AT US!

NOT SHOOTING AT *US*. SHOOTING AT *HER*.

I DON'T KNOW WHO HE WAS.

THE WHOLE TIME WE WERE INSIDE, NO ONE CARED ABOUT US.

YOU SHOW UP AND ALL OF A SUDDEN WE'RE BEING SHOT AT.

OLIVER'S RIGHT. IF SOMETHING IS GOING ON YOU SHOULD TELL US.

AND IF I KNEW I WOULD, BUT I DON'T SO I CAN'T.

YEAH, YOU ALREADY SAID THAT.

BECAUSE IT'S THE TRUTH!

I'D NEVER SEEN HIM UNTIL A FEW DAYS BEFORE I GOT SNAGGED BY A CHILD WELFARE SQUAD.

IT HAS TO HAVE SOMETHING TO DO WITH THE REGISTRY.

AGAIN WITH THE REGISTRY?!

IT'S A PIECE OF PAPER!

RRRRIP

AND IT WON'T EVER BRING THEM BACK!

I DON'T UNDERSTAND.

BEFORE THE DORMS I'D NEVER MET ANY OF YOU.

WHY WOULD MY FATHER BUY *YOU* GUYS ANYTHING?

OKAY, WELL, WE MUST HAVE SOME STUFF IN COMMON... WE'RE ALL ORPHANS.

WE ALL HAVE THE SAME REGISTRY.

THEY WERE ALL BOUGHT BY PHOEBE'S DAD.

AND THE DATE.

WHAT?

THE DATE ON ALL THE REGISTRIES IS 08/24/45.

THAT'S THE DAY BEFORE MY PARENTS DIED.

SAME HERE.

ME TOO.

YUP.

MINE, TOO.

I'VE LOOKED AT THIS THING OVER A MILLION TI--

I CAN'T BELIEVE I NEVER *REALIZED*...

MINE, TOO!

YOU GUYS DON'T--

DO YOU THINK THEY WERE, LIKE...

ALL TOGETHER? I MEAN, WHEN THEY DIED?

NO WAY.

IMPOSSIBLE.

MY PARENTS DIED IN A SHUTTLE ACCIDENT. IT'D BE MATHEMATICALLY IMPOSSIBLE FOR YOUR PARENTS TO HAVE ALSO DIED IN A--

THE CRAVEN SHUTTLE?

WHAT IF--

WHAT IF IT WASN'T AN ACCIDENT?

THE EXPLOSION, I MEAN. WHAT IF IT WASN'T AN ACCIDENT?

ALL THE PAPERS SAY THE SAME THING.

"A MECHANICAL FAILURE."

TWELVE BILLION DOLLARS.

THAT'S WHAT CRAVEN MINING COMPANY MADE LAST YEAR.

YOU WANNA KNOW HOW MANY ZEROS ARE IN TWELVE BILLION?

YOU THINK A NUMBER THAT BIG DOESN'T BUY YOU SOME FAVORS?

...

WE SHOULD PROBABLY FIND OUT WHAT'S ON THOSE MICROCHIPS.

STARTING TO TRUST ME YET?

I WAS WRONG. I'M SORRY. IF YOU WANT TO SAY "I TOLD YOU SO," GO AHEAD.

OLIVER, UNCOVERING A CONSPIRACY ABOUT THE DEATH OF OUR PARENTS WHILE SOME PSYCHO KILLER WORKING FOR THE LARGEST COMPANY IN THE UNIVERSE IS AFTER YOU ISN'T REALLY SOMETHING I WANTED TO BE RIGHT ABOUT.

NOW LET'S GET MOVING. LOOKS LIKE A STORM IS MOVING IN.

BUT APOLOGY ACCEPTED.

KZZZT.

MAIN COMPUTER BACK ONLINE.

FINALLY.

WHAT ARE YOU READING, STRICK?

NOTHING.

SAM, MY CAMERAS TELL ME YOU ARE IN FACT READING--

IT'S NOTHING. JUST GET WORKING ON THE NAV-SAT, OKAY?

S.O

WE'VE WASTED *ENOUGH* TIME OUT HERE.

MAN, THIS STORM CAME OUT OF NOWHERE!

IAN, LET'S GO!

WUMP!

MY REGISTRY!

WAP

WE HAVE TO GET IT!

ARE YOU CRAZY?

IF WE DON'T GET THAT REGISTRY BACK, THEY'RE ALL *USELESS!*

UH, THAT WAS A TREE THAT JUST FLEW PAST! IF ONE OF US GOES OUT THERE, WE'LL LAST *TWO SECONDS!*

THEN MAYBE WE *ALL* GO.

I SEE IT!

SNAP.

NOOOO!

THE NEXT MORNING.

WHAT NOW?

WE NEED TO FIND THAT REGISTRY.

YEAH, THAT SHOULD BE EASY. A MASSIVE MOON, A TINY PIECE OF PAPER. WHAT COULD BE THE PROBLEM THERE, RIGHT?

IT'S A METAL CHIP, RIGHT? MEANS WE CAN FIND IT WITH A METAL DETECTOR.

YOU DO KNOW WE DON'T HAVE A METAL DETECTOR, RIGHT?

I CAN MAKE ONE. FIFTH-GRADE SCIENCE FAIR.

YOU WON THE FIFTH-GRADE SCIENCE FAIR BY MAKING A METAL DETECTOR?

NO. JORDAN PLAINVIEW WON WITH HIS INTERACTIVE TIDE-POOL ECOSYSTEM.

I USED TWO HAIR DRYERS TO CREATE A CLASS-FOUR TORNADO. IT WAS COOL.

...UNTIL I ELECTROCUTED SYDNEY CORN'S IGUANA.

I CAME IN TWELFTH PLACE.

WHAT ABOUT THE *METAL DETECTOR*, OLIVER?!

OH, *RIGHT*. ALEXIS MARSCHENO TOOK THIRD PLACE BY MAKING A METAL DETECTOR.

I REMEMBER HOW.

LOOK, THAT MIGHT BE TRUE IN THEORY BUT THE CHIPS IN HERE ARE PRETTY SMALL.

REBECCA'S RIGHT. HOW CLOSE ARE WE GONNA HAVE TO GET TO THE CHIPS FOR THE METAL DETECTOR TO WORK?

WHAT IF WE HAD SOMETHING TO HELP US?

LIKE WHAT?

IT GLOWS, RIGHT? THE CHIP GLOWS. SO IT HAS A POWER SUPPLY. AND THE ONE THING ALL ENERGY SOURCES HAVE IN COMMON?

THEY GIVE OFF A SIGNAL!

AND IF IT GIVES OFF A SIGNAL, WE CAN TRACK IT!

GIVE THAT BOY A PRIZE!

BUT WHAT DO WE HAVE THAT CAN PICK UP A SIGNAL LIKE THAT?

THAT'S THE ONLY PROBLEM.

NOT NECESSARILY.

WHO KNOWS ANYTHING ABOUT BATS?

LATER

THE BEST PART...?

REMOTE CONTROL!!!

OKAY, SO WHICH WAY DO WE GO?

NORTH.

WHOA! HOLD ON!

WE COULD FIND THIS THING TOMORROW OR IT COULD TAKE YEARS. AND YOU WANNA KNOW THE **DIFFERENCE** BETWEEN THOSE TWO THINGS?

OUR FIRST STEP.

IF OUR FIRST STEP IS WRONG THEN EACH STEP THAT COMES AFTER IT IS ALSO WRONG.

SO, BEFORE WE JUST HEAD "NORTH" ALL WILLY-NILLY, I ASK YOU,

WHY NORTH?

'CAUSE THAT'S THE WAY THE STORM WAS BLOWING.

DUDE, WAY TO MAKE THE SILVER SIX PROUD.

UH, DOES ANYONE ELSE THINK THIS LOOKS--

THE DORM HOLOGRAM WALL, RIGHT?

TOTALLY.

I BET THIS ONE IS REAL.

HEY! THERE IT IS! THERE'S THE REGISTRY!

WHAT?

SERIOUSLY?

WHERE?!

I'M JOKING.

MY DAD USED TO DO THAT TO ME ALL THE TIME.

I HATED IT WHEN HE DID IT, BUT IT ALWAYS MADE ME SMILE.

UH, WHERE'S OLIVER?

OLIVER?!

MAYBE AN ANIMAL GOT HIM?!

ANIMAL? WHAT KIND OF ANIMAL?

I DON'T KNOW. SOME KIND OF KILLER MOON TIGER?

KILLER MOON TIGER?! IS THAT EVEN REAL?

I DON'T KNOW. MAYBE. I HOPE NOT.

AHHHHHHH!!!

94

YOU GUYS *HAAAAAVE* TO TRY THIS!

A LITTLE FUN? BREAK UP THE TENSION?

IT'S ALL GOOD, RIGHT?

NO...?

AAANND WE'RE DONE.

ANYTHING ON THE METER?

NOTHING.

WHAT NOW?

THERE.

SO... LIKE, WE'RE NOT CROSSING THAT, RIGHT?

NOPE.

WE GOT PLENTY OF PLACES TO LOOK FOR THE REGISTRY OVER HERE.

WE SHOULD MOVE OVER A SECTOR AND DOUBLE BACK, AND THEN--

...BE... ...EP... ...BEE... ...P...

...BE... ...EEEP... ...BEEEP.

IT COULD BE ANYTHING.

LIKE WHAT?

I DON'T KNOW. A METAL...

FLOWER?

A METAL FLOWER?

WE'RE CROSSING.

YOU COMING?

NO. I'LL STAY HERE. JUST IN CASE SOMETHING... HAPPENS.

OH, I FORGOT... THE BILLBOARD THING. YOU'RE SCARED OF HEIGHTS.

SCARED? NO. TERRIFIED? YES.

OKAY, LOOK. WE'LL CROSS TOGETHER.

JUST TAKE MY HAND AND WE'RE GONNA PRETEND WE'RE WALKING TO THE STORE, OKAY?

THE STORE?

YEAH.

WHAT KIND OF STORE?

THE SUPERMARKET.

WHY?

I DON'T KNOW. WE NEED MILK.

I'M LACTOSE INTOLERANT.

HOW'D YOU DO IT?

DO WHAT?

MANAGE TO STAY ON YOUR OWN FOR SO LONG?

I GOT LUCKY I GUESS.

I DOUBT IT. YOU'RE TOO SMART.

WHOA! HOLD EVERYTHING. A COMPLIMENT?

OF WHAT?

FINE. I WAS JEALOUS.

SOCIAL SERVICES BUSTED ME WITHIN ONE MONTH. YOU LASTED OVER A YEAR.

HOW'D THEY GET YOU?

I DECIDED TO COOK DINNER FOR MYSELF.

NO GIRLS ALLOWED!

TEN MINUTES LATER THE PLACE WAS IN FLAMES AND FIREFIGHTERS WERE EVERYWHERE.

FIVE MINUTES AFTER THAT, CHILD WELFARE AGENTS ARRIVED.

IF IT MAKES YOU FEEL ANY BETTER, IT GOT HARDER AND HARDER EVERY DAY.

AT LEAST YOU WERE *FREE.*

I DIDN'T *FEEL* FREE.

I FELT LIKE I WAS LIVING WITH A TARGET ON MY BACK. I COULDN'T TRUST ANYONE. I WENT TO SCHOOL AND BACK HOME.

AND ANY FRIENDS I *DID* HAVE, I HAD TO LIE TO.

YOU SLEPT IN YOUR OWN BED IN YOUR OWN HOUSE.

I WASN'T IN THE DORMS LIKE YOU GUYS, BUT I WASN'T FREE.

TRUE.

100

BEEP
BEEP

WE GOT SOMETHING!

WHERE DO YOU THINK?

I'M NOT SURE, BUT IT'S CLOSE...

MAX, LIGHT.

BEEP BEEP BEEP

BEEP
BEEP
BEEP
BEEP

WHAT IS IT?

WELL, NOW WE KNOW ONE THING.

WHAT?

WE WEREN'T THE FIRST ONES HERE.

NEVER SEEN ANYTHING LIKE IT BEFORE.

THERE'S A BUTTON.

PUSH IT.

WE PUSH IT AND *ANYTHING* CAN HAPPEN.

HEY!

WHERE ARE *YOU* GOING?

ME?
JUST OVER THERE,
BEHIND THAT DUNE.

IN CASE THAT'S A BOMB,
WHICH I'M SURE IT ISN'T--

-- EVEN THOUGH THAT'S
EXACTLY WHAT IT LOOKS LIKE!

CLICK

SOMEONE PLEASE
TELL ME THAT'S
WHAT I THINK
IT IS.

TING

MAX?

IT WASN'T ME! I SWEAR!

IT'S FAINT...

...BUT IT'S PICKING UP SOMETHING.

DUE EAST.

OH, BOY...

TELL ME WE'RE NOT CROSSING THIS ONE....

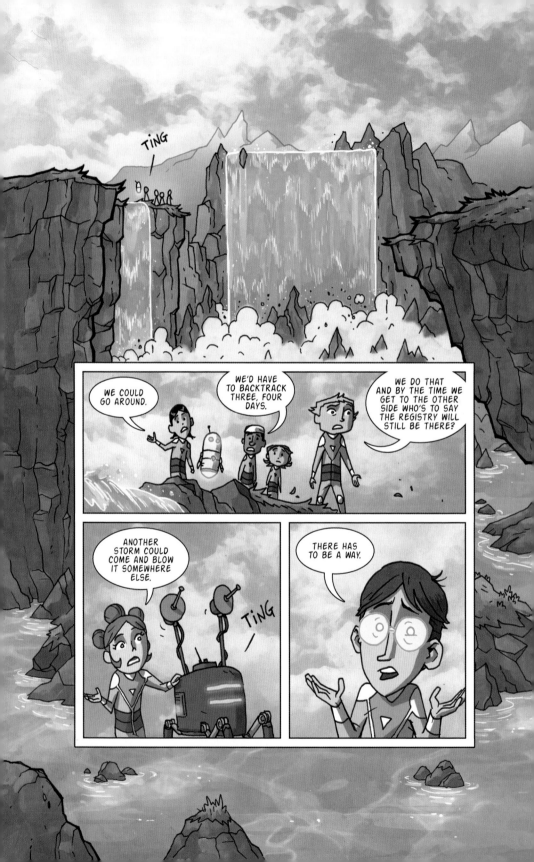

PHOEBE, CAN I TELL YOU SOMETHING?

HMM...

WHEN MY FOLKS DIED, I THOUGHT MY LIFE COULDN'T GET ANY WORSE. AND THEN AFTER I GOT SENT TO THE DORMS I REALIZED I WAS WRONG.

I NEVER THOUGHT ABOUT TRYING TO GET OUT. NOT UNTIL YOU SHOWED UP.

HEY, WE'RE THE SILVER SIX, RIGHT?

YOU KNOW WHAT I THINK I LIKE MOST OUT HERE?

THE STARS SEEM SO CLOSE.

ESPECIALLY THAT ONE!

SEE IT?

WHERE?

SEE THE BRANCH, WHERE THE LEAVES LOOK KINDA LIKE AN OLD MAN WHO JUST ATE A SLICE OF LEMON.

TH-THAT'S NOT A ST--

OH, MY!

...WE FOUND IT.

WE FOUND THE REGISTRY! IT'S IN THE TREE!

WHAT IS IT?

A SUBMICRO NANO-CHIP.

CAN YOU FIND OUT WHAT'S ON IT?

SURE.

IF I HAD A COMPUTER THAT WAS SIX GENERATIONS OLD.

WHAT? WE CAME ALL THIS WAY FOR *NOTHING?!*

THIS CHIP IS ABOUT FIFTEEN YEARS OLD.

IT WON'T WORK IN ANYTHING I HAVE.

I NEED SOMETHING A LOT MORE...

...CRAPPY.

WHAT?

WAIT. HOLD ON...

YOU'RE SAYING THAT ONCE WE DOWNLOAD WHATEVER IS ON THAT CHIP, MAX IS GOING TO BE WIPED CLEAN?

COMPLETELY.

SO... HE WON'T REMEMBER WHO I AM?

OR REMEMBER ANYTHING ABOUT YOUR LIFE.

HE'S GOING TO... DIE?

I-I GUESS... IN A WAY, YES.

I CAN'T-- I WON'T...

WE HAVE TO FIND ANOTHER WAY.

PHOEBE, WE CAN'T--

NO!

HE'S FAMILY!

HE'S ALL I HAVE!

PHOEBE--

THAT'S NOT TRUE.

115

I KNOW.

PHOEBE, YOU DIDN'T HAVE A CHOICE.

BUT IT DOESN'T HELP, RIGHT?

NOT EVEN A LITTLE.

WE DON'T HAVE TO WATCH IT NOW. I MEAN, WE CAN WAIT. I MEAN... WE SHOULD WAIT.

NO.

LET'S DO IT NOW.

WE'RE TAKING THIS PRECAUTION BECAUSE IT'S OUR BELIEF WE'VE LOCATED THE POSSIBLE SOURCE OF A NEW TYPE OF FUEL.

SOMETHING THAT WOULD REPLACE HYDRO-2.

HEY, I SEE MY FOLKS!

AND MINE!

YOU GET TO THE GOOD NEWS YET?

NO.

OUR PROBLEM--

AND IT'S A BIG ONE.

--OUR PROBLEM IS THAT ALL OUR EXPERIMENTS UP TO THIS POINT HAVE FAILED.

WE SEEM TO BE MISSING AN ELEMENT.

WE'RE AMAZINGLY CLOSE TO A BREAKTHROUGH, BUT WE'RE RUNNING OUT OF TIME.

BUT ONCE WE FIGURE OUT WHAT THIS MISSING LINK IS, WE'LL HAVE DISCOVERED THE VERY THING THAT WILL MAKE HYDRO-2 OBSOLETE.

YOU SAY ANYTHING ABOUT CRAVEN YET?

NO.

WE'RE SEEING HIM TOMORROW.

DID YOUR DAD JUST SAY THEY WERE SEEING CRAVEN?

HE DID, YES.

WE'VE BEEN TRYING FOR MONTHS, AND YUKI YOSHIYAMA JUST HEARD MR. CRAVEN HAS FINALLY AGREED TO SEE US.

OUR HOPE IS THAT WE CAN CONVINCE HIM TO FUND THE REST OF OUR RESEARCH.

THE OTHERS THINK I'M BEING NAIVE.

YOU *ARE*.

AND *YOU'RE* TOO CYNICAL!

THAT'S WHY YOU MARRIED ME.

THE GOAL IS TO PROVE TO CRAVEN THAT BEING THE RICHEST MAN IN THE WORLD MEANS VERY LITTLE IF THE WORLD IS A DESOLATE WASTELAND.

JOHN, HE DOESN'T CARE. WE SHOULD GO PUBLIC. TALK TO THE PRESS. PUT PRESSURE ON CRAVEN.

I THINK WE NEED CRAVEN. HIS MONEY, HIS RESOURCES. I THINK...

I HOPE...

CRAVEN CAN STILL BE CONVINCED.

HE'S GOING TO WANT TO KNOW WHERE THIS PLACE IS, JOHN.

I KNOW.

AND WE CAN'T TELL HIM. EDEN-2 HAS TO REMAIN A SECRET UNTIL WE KNOW WHAT WE'VE FOUND HERE REALLY WORKS.

WE CAN'T TRUST CRAVEN. NOT YET.

I-- WE NEED TO MEET HIM. FACE-TO-FACE.

THEN WE'LL KNOW IF WE CAN TRUST HIM. AT LEAST WE KNOW EDEN-2 WILL STAY SAFE.

■ RECORDING STOPPED

WHEN WAS THIS RECORDED?

AUGUST 24TH, 7:57 P.M....

THE 24TH? THAT'S THE DAY BEFORE THE SHUTTLE ACCIDENT!

RECORDING STOPPED

THEY WENT TO SEE CRAVEN THE DAY THEY DIED.

GUYS, WAIT. THERE'S MORE.

SINCE WE'RE UNSURE WHEN WE'LL GET A CHANCE TO RETURN TO EDEN-2 WE'VE DECIDED TO STRIP OUR SHIP OF EVERYTHING WE CAN SO WE CAN BRING BACK AS MANY SOIL SAMPLES AS POSSIBLE.

AN ADVANCED DEGREE IN ASTROPHYSICS, AND LOOK, I'M MOVING BOXES OF FREEZE-DRIED FRUIT.

WHAT'S THIS?

A SIGNAL BEACON.

PUSH THAT BUTTON AND IT RELAYS ITS COORDINATES TO THE NEAREST CRAVEN PROBE.

KEEP IT OR TOSS IT?

TOSS IT. WE DON'T NEED--

PLAYBACK COMPLETE

THAT'S IT. IT'S OVER.

I DON'T KNOW! GET CRAVEN?! TURN HIM IN! WE CAN'T JUST LET HIM GET AWAY WITH THIS!

OLIVER, THERE'S LITTLE WE CAN DO.

AT LEAST HERE WE'RE SAFE.

BESIDES, MOST BILLIONAIRE PSYCHOS? NOT ALL THAT NICE.

SO THAT'S IT? WE JUST FORGET HE *MURDERED* OUR PARENTS?!

NO. WE DON'T FORGET. WE WAIT.

DO YOU HEAR THIS? TALK TO THEM!

MAYBE THEY'RE RIGHT. THIS IS OUR HOME NOW. BEEN A LONG TIME SINCE I COULD SAY THAT.

WE'RE SAFE AS LONG AS CRAVEN DOESN'T KNOW WE'RE--

RRRRRUUUMMBLE.

THIS CAN'T BE GOOD.

IT MIGHT NOT BE AS BAD AS IT SEEMS.

REALLY? 'CAUSE IT SEEMS PRETTY BAD.

CRAVEN MUST HAVE THOUSANDS OF THESE PROBES THROUGHOUT THE GALAXY.

YEAH, BUT ONLY ONE WAS CALLED HERE BY US.

THAT'S NOT THE ONLY PROBLEM.

THE MINUTE WE PUSHED THE BUTTON ON THAT SIGNAL BEACON--

--A COMPUTER SOMEWHERE REGISTERED A DISTRESS CALL FROM A SHIP THAT BLEW UP A YEAR AGO!

BECCA, HOW MUCH TIME DO YOU THINK WE HAVE BEFORE THE PROBE BOOTS UP?

SAT-NAV SYSTEMS FOR THIS MODEL? MAYBE AN HOUR.

Whirrrr

OF COURSE, I COULD BE WRONG.

LET'S JUST *BREAK* IT. KIDS BREAK THINGS ALL THE TIME, RIGHT?

THERE ARE SIX OF US! HOW LONG COULD IT TAKE?

NO. THIS MOON IS OURS.

I'VE LOST ONE HOME, I'M *NOT* LOSING ANOTHER.

THIS IS OUR *HOME!*

KLANG

KLANG

KLANG KLANG KLANG

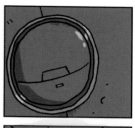

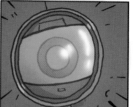

130

WHAT ABOUT NOW?

GOOD.

OKAY, RUN A SYSTEM CHECK AND START SWEEPING THE AREA BY QUADRANT.

WHAT ARE WE LOOKING FOR?

ANYTHING OUT OF THE ORDINARY.

LIKE A PROBE BEING PULLED OFF ITS TRAJECTORY BY A DECOMMISSIONED SIGNAL BEACON?

YEAH, I GUESS.

NO, I MEAN I JUST FOUND THAT.

WHAT? WHERE?

COMING ON-SCREEN NOW.

CAN YOU REMOTE-HACK THE PROBE'S HARD DRIVE?

WHAT DO YOU THINK?

132

RATA TATA TAT

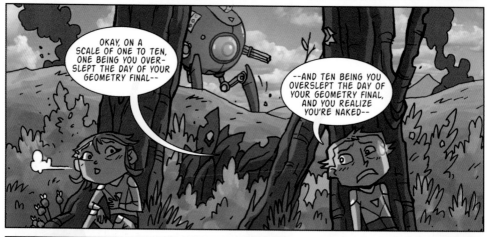

OKAY, ON A SCALE OF ONE TO TEN, ONE BEING YOU OVER-SLEPT THE DAY OF YOUR GEOMETRY FINAL--

--AND TEN BEING YOU OVERSLEPT THE DAY OF YOUR GEOMETRY FINAL, AND YOU REALIZE YOU'RE NAKED--

--AND INSTEAD OF HANDS YOU HAVE, LIKE, CRAZY PENGUIN FLIPPERS, SO YOU CAN'T HOLD A PEN ANYWAY...

WHAT'S THIS?

ABOUT AN EIGHTEEN.

ABSOLUTELY NOT.

BAD IDEA.

MASSIVELY BAD.

COLOSSALLY BAD.

PHOEBE, SOCIAL SERVICES ARE WAITING FOR EACH ONE OF US. WE GO BACK, THAT'S IT. LIFE AS WE KNOW IT IS OVER.

THEN I'LL GO.

WHAT?!

I'M THE ONE THEY WANT. THEY DON'T KNOW ABOUT YOU GUYS.

THAT AGENT SAW US BUST OUT OF THE DORMS WITH YOU.

I COULD HAVE LET YOU OUT ANYWHERE.

THEN WHAT WILL *WE* DO?

STOP THE PROBE.

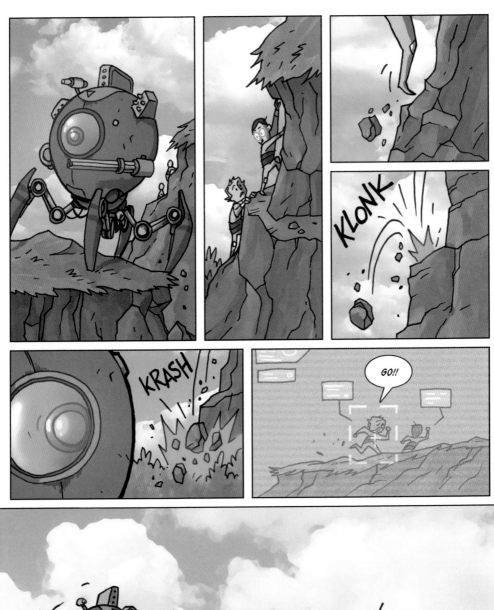

KEEP LOW AND QUIET.

CRACK

YOU WANT TO GO NEXT?

I'M GOOD.

YOU OKAY?

NOT EVEN A LITTLE.

PHOEBE!

BLAM

OLIVER!

WAS IT YOU?

WAS IT ME WHAT?

WERE YOU THE ONE WHO KILLED OUR PARENTS?

ANYONE EVER TELL YOU THAT IT'S IMPOLITE TO ASK SOMEONE IF THEY KILLED YOUR PARENTS?

REALLY? YOU'RE GOING TO *PATRONIZE* ME NOW?

YOU HAVE *NO* IDEA WHAT MY FRIENDS AND I HAVE BEEN THROUGH!

ACTUALLY, YOU'D BE *VERY* SURPRISED AT WHAT I KNOW ABOUT WHAT YOU'VE BEEN THROUGH!

AND *NO*, I DID NOT KILL YOUR PARENTS.

BUT YOU KNOW WHO DID?

WHAT WERE YOU DOING ALL THE WAY OUT HERE?

TRYING TO SAVE THE WORLD.

NOT THAT *YOU'D* CARE.

REALLY?

MY PARENTS WERE *THIS* CLOSE TO SOLVING THE WORLD'S ENERGY PROBLEM.

AND YOU AND YOUR FRIENDS THOUGHT YOU COULD FINISH THE JOB?

THOUGHT? WE *WILL*.

IT MIGHT TAKE A LOT LONGER, BUT WE'RE NOT GIVING UP TILL WE DO!

SO YOU CAN TELL YOUR BOSS THAT SOONER OR LATER WE'RE GOING TO PUT HIM OUT OF BUSINESS!

WHAT NOW?

WE SAVE PHOEBE.

HOW? THE SHIP'S FUEL CELLS ARE EMPTY! WE CAN'T GO ANYWHERE.

BESIDES, IT'S NOT WHAT SHE WANTED. SHE SAID WE SHOULD STAY HERE, STOP THE PROBE.

THAT WAS BEFORE THE PROBE STARTED TRYING TO KILL US!

TECHNICALLY, IT HAD ALREADY STARTED TO TRY AND KILL US.

WHERE ARE WE GOING TO GET A CHARGE STRONG ENOUGH TO DO *THAT?*

WHATEVER! OLIVER'S RIGHT. WE NEED TO FIGURE OUT HOW TO RECHARGE THE TRANSPORT SHIP.

THAT'S IT! WE USE THE PROBE!

FOR WHAT?

TO RECHARGE THE SHIP'S FUEL CELLS.

IF WE USE THE SHOCK ABSORBING PANELS FROM THE SHIP WE CAN HARNESS THE ENERGY FROM THE BLAST.

WHOA! YOU WANT THE PROBE TO **INTENTIONALLY** FIRE A ROCKET AT US?!

AND THEN WHAT? JUST STAND THERE?

YEAH. WE CAN REROUTE THE ENERGY INTO OUR FUEL CELLS.

IT SHOULD WORK.

...WHAT DO YOU MEAN, "SHOULD WORK"?

146

2.35%

FUEL CELL
ENERGY LEVEL

DID IT
WORK?

TOTALLY!
THAT WAS
AMAZING!

IAN,
PHASE TWO
IS A GO!

100.5%

FUEL CELL
ENERGY LEVEL

IAN, YOU OKAY?

OKAY? DID YOU NOT *SEE* WHAT I JUST *DID?!* I'M *GREAT!* THAT WAS *AWESOME!*

FUEL CELLS ARE CHARGED! WE'RE GOOD TO GO!

YOU BROUGHT HER HERE?!

OF *ALL* THE PLACES TO BRING HER, YOU BRING HER TO THE *COMPANY HEADQUARTERS?!*

WHY?

SHE TOLD ME WHAT HER PARENTS WERE DOING AND I THOUGHT--

I DON'T PAY YOU TO *THINK!* IT'S *NOT* WHAT YOU DO BEST!

AND WHAT IS IT I DO BEST?

TAKE ORDERS.

YOU SHOULD LISTEN TO HER. SHE HAS A LOT OF GOOD IDEAS.

SHE COULD HELP.

HELP WHO?

EVERYONE. US. THE COMPANY. SOONER OR LATER HYDRO-2 WILL--

YOU THINK SHE'S GOING TO FORGET WHAT WE DID TO HER PARENTS?

SAM, SHE'S THE ONLY ONE WHO CAN CONNECT US TO THAT SHUTTLE EXPLOSION. SHE HAS TO...

DISAPPEAR.

YOU WANT ME TO... KILL HER?!

I WANT YOU TO DO WHATEVER'S NECESSARY TO HELP THIS COMPANY!

BUT SHE'S A KID.

AFTER EVERYTHING I'VE DONE FOR YOU.

EVERYTHING I GAVE YOU.

SAY IT. WHAT DID I DO FOR YOU?

SAY IT!

YOU... YOU SAVED ME.

THAT'S RIGHT. AND DON'T *EVER* FORGET IT.

SAM, SHE'S JUST AN ORPHAN. NO ONE CARES WHAT HAPPENS TO HER, RIGHT?

...RIGHT.

MAKE ME PROUD.

WHOA! WAIT!!

YOU DON'T WANT TO DO THIS!

SAM! IT'S SAM, RIGHT? YOUR NAME IS SAM?

JUST TELL ME ONE THING, SAM--

IS CRAVEN, LIKE, YOUR DAD?

THIS IS *SO* NOT GOING TO WORK.

IAN, RELAX. IF WE GET STOPPED JUST FOLLOW MY LEAD.

CRAVEN COMPOUND A-1

HEY! YOU KIDS!

WHERE DO YOU THINK YOU'RE GOING?

THIS IS THE DEEP-DRILLING AREA, RIGHT?

YEAH, SO, WHAT ABOUT IT?

WE'RE YOUR NEW CREW.

WHERE DO YOU WANT US?

OKAY... BE READY AND STEADY IN TEN.

DEEP DRILLING? WHERE'D THAT COME FROM?

WHEN MY FATHER FIRST STARTED AT CRAVEN, THAT'S WHERE HE WORKED.

WHERE IS EVERYBODY?

IT'S SATURDAY.

REALLY?

OKAY, THE PROBE'S REPORT HAS BEEN LOGGED. OUR MOON IS... RIGHT HERE.

WHERE SHOULD WE PUT IT?

MAYBE WE SHOULDN'T. MAYBE WE SHOULD ERASE IT.

PATEL'S RIGHT. IF WE MOVE IT, SOMEONE MIGHT STUMBLE OVER IT.

IF WE *ERASE* IT, IT'S GONE FOR *GOOD*.

POINT TAKEN.

WHAT'S NEXT?

PHOEBE.

WOW, THIS JUST GETS BETTER AND BETTER.

THEY WITH YOU?

YEAH.

I CAN'T BELIEVE WE FOUND YOU!

YOU STOPPED THE PROBE?

YEAH.

WHAT'S YOUR NAME?

STRICK, SAM OWEN STRICK.

YOU KILL OUR PARENTS, SAM STRICK?

OLIVER, NO! DON'T!

I WANT TO KNOW IF HE HAD ANYTHING TO DO WITH THE SHUTTLE EXPLOSION!

I DIDN'T. BUT I COULD'VE DONE MORE.

I SHOULD'VE DONE MORE.

WHAT DOES *THAT* MEAN?

SAM...

SAM STRICK...

SAM OWEN STRICK... S, O....

S. O.... S.

IT'S HIM! IT HAS TO BE!

IT'S YOU! S.O.S.! YOU'RE THE KID WITH THE--

WE NEED TO FIND HIM!

WHAT? WE GOTTA GO. NOW.

WE CAN'T. NOT YET. YOU KNOW THE DORM HALLWAY WITH ALL THE INITIALS ON IT?

YEAH, WE ALL SIGNED IT.

WELL, SO DID STRICK!

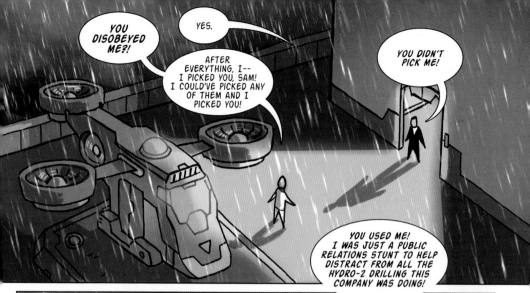

JUST SO I'M STRAIGHT-- THAT'S THE PROBE, RIGHT?

UH-HUH.

RATA TAT TAT TAT TAT

I THOUGHT YOU GUYS TOOK CARE OF THE PROBE!!

IT MUST HAVE TRACKED OUR SHUTTLE BACK HERE!

TAT TAT TAT

GET OUT!

WHO KNOWS HOW TO FLY THIS THING?

...

OKAY, NEXT TIME LET'S *NOT* GET RID OF THE PILOT UNTIL WE KNOW THIS KINDA STUFF.

BEEP BEEP
BEEP HONK

VROOM

INITIATE
SCAN--

--SAMUEL
OWEN
STRICK

crvn#0013

20X

?!

WHAT'S
IT DOING?!

COMING
BACK.
FOR US!

NO.

KA-BOOM!

THAT'S IT. I'M DONE PLAYING WITH THIS PILE OF JUNK.

WE NEED TO SPLIT UP.

WHOA, WHAT?!

YEAH, THE LAST TIME WE SPLIT UP NOTHING GOOD HAPPENED.

IT'S THE ONLY WAY.

AS LONG AS I'M WITH YOU, YOU'RE ALL IN DANGER.

YOU GUYS FIND A SHIP TO GET US BACK HOME. THEN GET ANY SUPPLIES WE'LL NEED.

I'LL MEET YOU BEHIND THE STRATFORD ROAD SCHOOL TONIGHT.

WHAT ARE YOU GONNA DO?

RUN.

PRIMARY TARGET

TRACKING...

ADJUSTING SPEED...

FAST.

:ZOOM 50X

HEY--

WHAT ARE YOU DOING?!

YOU THINK I'M GONNA LET YOU HAVE ALL THE FUN?

WE HAVE A PLAN OR WE JUST WINGING IT?

A LITTLE BIT OF BOTH.

BOOM

THIS BUS IS OUT OF SERVICE. PLEASE EXIT IMMEDIATELY.

WE GOTTA MOVE. WE'RE SITTING DUCKS.

YOU SHOULD GO, OLIVER.

WHAT?

YOU SHOULD GO. WHILE YOU CAN.

PHOEBE, THAT MOON IS THE FIRST PLACE TO FEEL LIKE HOME TO ME IN--

I'M NOT LETTING IT GO WITHOUT DOING EVERYTHING I CAN TO PROTECT IT!

BESIDES, THE SILVER SIX NEEDS YOU.

...OKAY, BUT--

YOU PROMISE ME SOMETHING?

YEAH, OF COURSE. ANYTHING.

DON'T FOLLOW ME.

I WANT MY HOME BACK!

AMAZING!

COUGH.

IT'S ABSOLUTELY *AMAZING* WHAT FALLS FROM THE SKY THESE DAYS.

AND YOU KNOW WHAT'S MORE AMAZING?

THIS REPORT YOUR PARENTS PUT TOGETHER.

W-WHERE'D YOU GET THAT?!

YOUR FRIENDS.

THEY HAD NOTHING! YOUR PARENTS HAD NOTHING!

THEY NEVER FOUND THE MISSING ELEMENT!

THEY! FAILED!

BUT WE WON'T!

WE'RE GONNA TELL EVERYONE!

TELL EVERYONE WHAT?

THE TRUTH!

YOU KILLED OUR PARENTS AND YOU KEPT THE POSSIBILITY OF A NEW FUEL SOURCE SECRET, ALL SO YOU COULD MAKE MORE MONEY WITH HYDRO-2.

YOU HAVE ANY PROOF OF THAT?

WE HAVE THE REPORT!

NO... I HAVE THE REPORT.

WE HAVE THE TRUTH!

ONCE I GET DONE, EVEN YOU SIX WON'T KNOW THE TRUTH ANYMORE.

WE HAVE THE MOON.

NOT FOR LONG.

WHAT DOES THAT MEAN?

I'M GOING TO TELL YOU A COMPANY SECRET...

CRAVEN MINING COMPANY JUST BOUGHT A SMALL WEAPONS MANUFACTURER.

THEIR SPECIALTY?

MISSILES.

GUIDED MISSILES.

THAT'S OUR HOME!

NOT ANYMORE.

YOU'RE GOING TO *PAY* FOR THAT! I DON'T KNOW HOW OR WHEN, BUT YOU WILL!

I *HIGHLY* DOUBT IT.

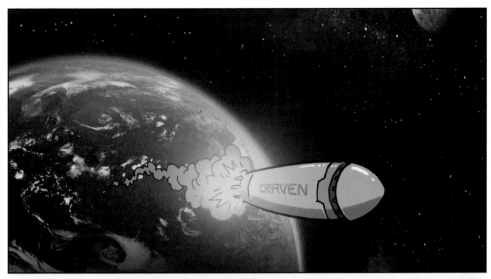

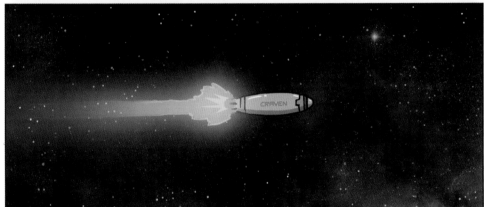

HEY, OLIVER, WORD IS THAT WHEN THEY FINALLY BUSTED YOU GUYS--

--YOU WERE ALL SITTING IN A POLICE CRUISER... A *STOLEN* POLICE CRUISER--

S.O.S.

--WHICH YOU CRASHED INTO A DAIRY DUKE--

--WHERE YOU GUYS GOT TO EAT ALL THE FREE ICE CREAM YOU COULD SHOVE INTO YOUR MOUTHS!

SO, THAT TRUE?!

TWENTY-SIX GALLONS!

GO. AWAY.

178

HEY, OLIVER, CHECK THIS OUT! YOU GUYS ARE ON TV!

...TURN IT UP!!

...A DISCOVERY THAT ASTROPHYSICISTS ARE CALLING A MODERN-DAY MIRACLE.

IT STARTED THREE WEEKS AGO, WHEN WHAT ASTRONOMERS CALL AN ORPHAN MOON EXPLODED IN DEEP SPACE.

ALTHOUGH UNCONFIRMED, EARLY REPORTS INDICATE THAT THIS EXPLOSION FUSED THE CHEMICAL ELEMENTS SPECIFIC TO THIS RARE MOON, CREATING A NEW TYPE OF FUEL.

FOR MORE ON THIS STORY LET'S CHECK IN WITH BROCK JAMES. BROCK?

news @11

JIM NASIUM

ocodile found in sewer system -- Man steals his own money -- Hydro-2 shares

THANKS, JIM. I'M HERE OUTSIDE THE INTERNATIONAL ASTRONOMY UNION, THE GOVERNING BODY OF ALL SPACE.

INCREDIBLY, EARLY REPORTS HAVE TOP RESEARCHERS SAYING THIS NEW FUEL SOURCE CAN AND WILL END OUR CRIPPLING DEPENDENCY ON HYDRO-2.

BELIEVE IT OR NOT, JIM, IT WAS A CLASS-V ULTRASONIC MISSILE.

AMAZING, JUST AMAZING.

BROCK, DO WE KNOW WHAT CAUSED THE EXPLOSION?

BROCK JAMES
International Astronomy Union

THAT'S NOT ALL. RUMORS ARE RAMPANT THAT RESEARCHERS HAVE DISCOVERED AN OBJECT ON THE REMAINS OF THIS ORPHAN MOON.

NO ONE SEEMS TO KNOW WHAT IT IS OR WHAT PART IT PLAYED IN THESE EVENTS, BUT WE DO KNOW THIS:

IT'S AN OBJECT THE GOVERNMENT THINKS IS CRUCIAL TO THEIR INVESTIGATION--

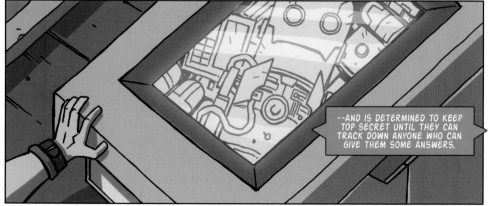

--AND IS DETERMINED TO KEEP TOP SECRET UNTIL THEY CAN TRACK DOWN ANYONE WHO CAN GIVE THEM SOME ANSWERS.

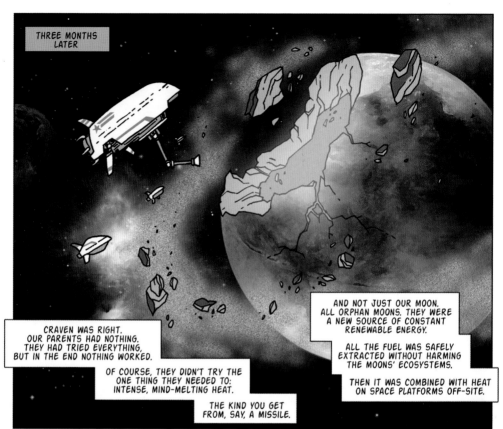

THREE MONTHS LATER

CRAVEN WAS RIGHT. OUR PARENTS HAD NOTHING. THEY HAD TRIED EVERYTHING, BUT IN THE END NOTHING WORKED.

OF COURSE, THEY DIDN'T TRY THE ONE THING THEY NEEDED TO: INTENSE, MIND-MELTING HEAT.

THE KIND YOU GET FROM, SAY, A MISSILE.

AND NOT JUST OUR MOON. ALL ORPHAN MOONS. THEY WERE A NEW SOURCE OF CONSTANT RENEWABLE ENERGY.

ALL THE FUEL WAS SAFELY EXTRACTED WITHOUT HARMING THE MOONS' ECOSYSTEMS.

THEN IT WAS COMBINED WITH HEAT ON SPACE PLATFORMS OFF-SITE.

ALMOST IMMEDIATELY THE STEEL BUBBLES STARTED TO COME DOWN, ONE BY ONE, THE WORLD OVER.

FOR THE FIRST TIME WE HAD PARKS AND WOODS, AND THERE WAS SPACE.

OLIVER SAID IT BEST WHEN HE TOLD CRAVEN THAT SOMEHOW, SOME WAY, HE WAS GOING TO PAY.

AND THOUGH WE HAD NO IDEA HOW...

GUILTY.

CRAVEN DID PAY. AND IT COST HIM EVERYTHING.

AND THE SILVER SIX?

WE WERE HEROES.

WORLDWIDE, ROCK-STAR-LEVEL HEROES.

AND YOU WANNA KNOW THE BEST THING ABOUT BEING A HERO? ALL THE PEOPLE THAT WANT TO MEET YOU.

ONE WAS NAMED GRACE. SHE WAS VERY COOL.

AND VERY POWERFUL.

THE WORD *REWARD* DOESN'T EVEN BEGIN TO COVER IT BUT I'LL ASK ANYWAY:

OF ALL THE THINGS YOU WANT, WHAT IS IT YOU WANT MOST?

OUR HOME. WE WANT OUR HOME BACK.

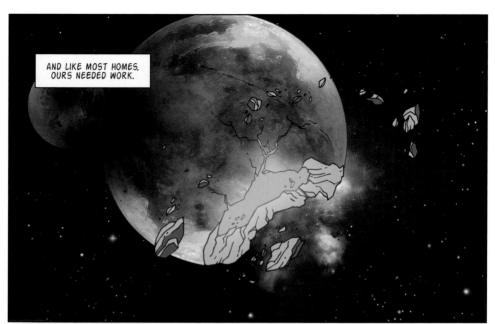

AND LIKE MOST HOMES, OURS NEEDED WORK.

YOU THINK IT'LL WORK?

PHOEBE, I DON'T-- YOU SHOULDN'T GET YOUR HOPES UP.

NO. RIGHT. OF COURSE.

BUT THERE IS A CHANCE HE COULD REMEMBER, RIGHT?

PHOEBS, AFTER ALL HE'S BEEN THROUGH, THE ODDS OF HIM REMEMBERING ANYTHING ARE, LIKE...

INFINITESIMAL.

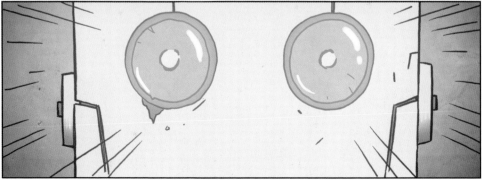